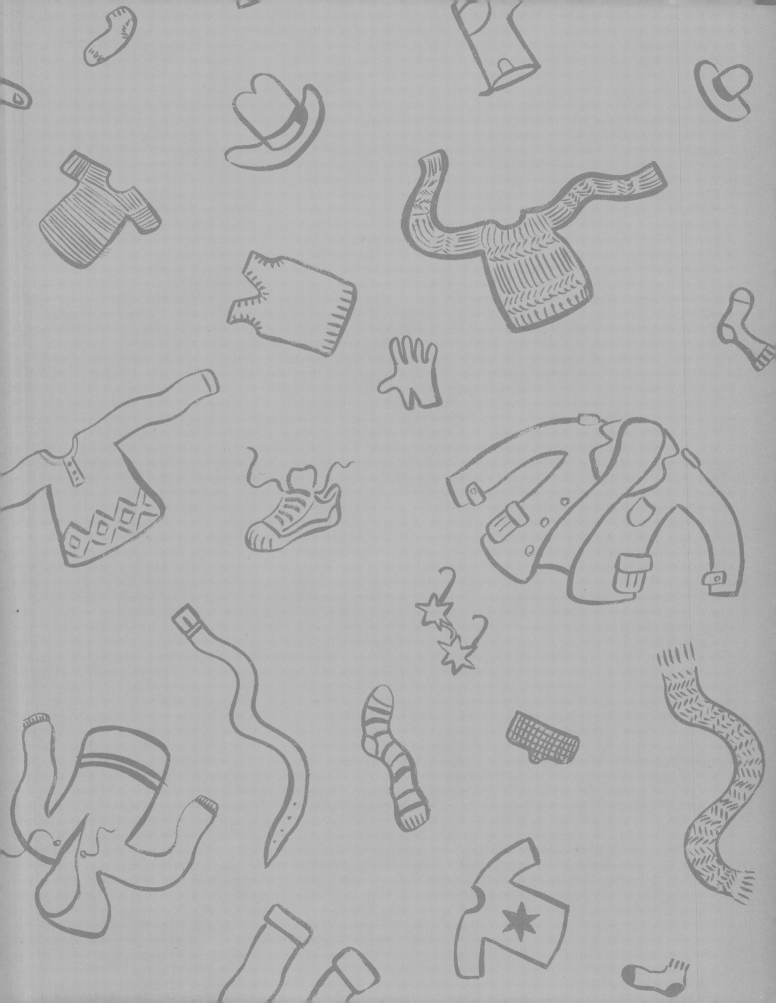

To Superrrr Naked Mannnn!!!!!!!!

Bloomsbury Publishing, London, New Delhi, New York and Sydney

First published in Great Britain in 2008 by Fizzbomb Books Ltd.
This paperback edition published in 2013 by Bloomsbury Publishing Plc
50 Bedford Square, London, WC1B 3DP

Text copyright © Fizzbomb Books Ltd. 2008, 2013
Illustrations copyright © Garry Parsons 2008
The moral rights of the author and illustrator have been asserted

A CIP catalogue record for this book is available from the British Library

ISBN 978 1 4088 3659 0

Printed in China

1 3 5 7 9 10 8 6 4 2

All papers used by Bloomsbury Publishing are natural, recyclable products made from
wood grown in well-managed forests. The manufacturing processes conform to the
environmental regulations of the country of origin

www.bloomsbury.com

NUDDY NED

Kes Gray and Garry Parsons

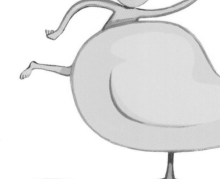

BLOOMSBURY

LONDON NEW DELHI NEW YORK SYDNEY

Busy in the bedroom,
Making up Ned's bed,
There was Mum and there was Dad...

But **where** was Nuddy Ned?

Ned was in the bathroom,
Standing on the mat,
all clean and fresh and sparkling.
Thank bubble bath for that!

Ned looked in the mirror,
And did a little **wiggle.**
He waved his arms and jumped about . . .

And **then** began to **giggle.**

His heart filled up with **naughtiness**,
His eyes began to flash.

He did a **hop** and then a **skip**,
And then he made a dash.

"Yahoo!" said Ned. "Waahey!" said Ned,
"They don't teach this at school.
Life is far more interesting
With nothing on at all."

Ned did **nuddy cartwheels,**
And star jumps **willy-nilly.**

He'd never felt so **loopy-loo.**

He'd never been so **silly.**

"Put some clothes on! Get dressed now!
Ned, don't you be so bold!"
Ned's mum and dad were **not** impressed,
But Ned would **not** be told.

Ned leapt across the sofa,
And raced into the hall.
Then charged out through the front door,
With nothing on at all!

Ned **scooted** past the rose beds,
And **jumped** the garden gate.
He **hurtled** on his nuddy way.
(Nuddiness won't wait!)

"I'm Nuddy Ned! I'm Nuddy Ned!
Jim-jams aren't for me!
I'm never wearing clothes again.
It's the nuddy life for me!"

His mum and dad chased after him,
Gasping, wheezing, puffing.
All the neighbours stood and stared,
"Good grief, Ned's wearing **nothing!**"

Ned ran past and waved at them,
"Good evening! Lovely weather!
How do you like my latest look?
It's called **the altogether!**"

Ned cartwheeled past the bus stop,
And sprang his big surprise.
Late night shoppers dropped their bags,
And covered up their eyes.

Down the high street, through the park,
Nuddy Ned ran riot.
"Put some clothes on!" people cried.
"I won't!" said Ned...

"Be quiet!"

Ned raced through the precinct,
In his birthday suit.
His mum and dad chased after him,
In hot but tired pursuit.

"Nuddy Ned! Nuddy Ned!
Don't you be so rude!
Don't go in the pizza house.
You'll put them off their food!"

The pizza topping counter,
Is precisely where Ned sat.
"Good evening ladies and gentlemen.
I'm Nuddy Ned. Top that!"

People screamed and hid their eyes,
With deep-pan pizza crusts.
Ned skidaddled through the door,
And ran to catch a bus.

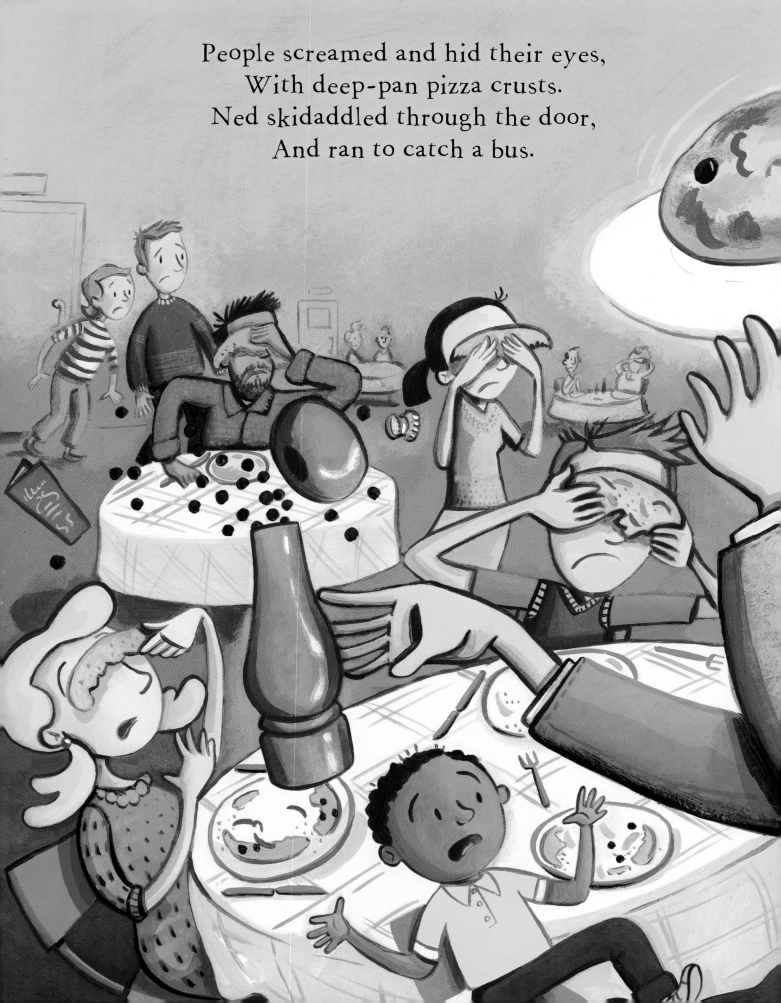

The bus conductor
shook his fist,

"Get off my bus!" he freaked,
"You'll have to walk..."

"Or run!" laughed Ned.
"Or – even better – streak!"

Nuddy Ned leapt off the bus,
And jumped a six foot fence.
He landed in a field of cows,
Who haven't felt right since.

His mum and dad climbed after him,
And fell into a heap.

"We'll never catch him in these fields . . .
Not even with a jeep."

"Ned come back! It's rather rude,
To run round in the nuddy!"
"It's not!" said Ned. "It's monster fun!
Don't be so fuddy-duddy!"

Ned's mum and dad sat on the grass.
Was it really worth this fuss?
"Perhaps he's right? We could find out . . ."

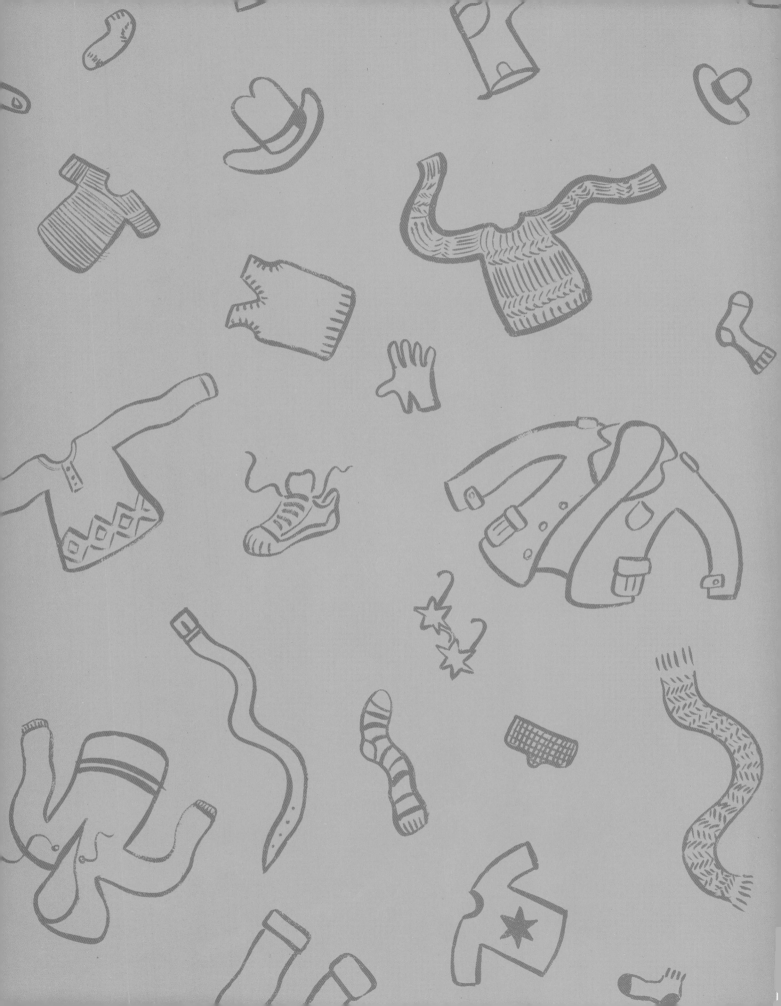

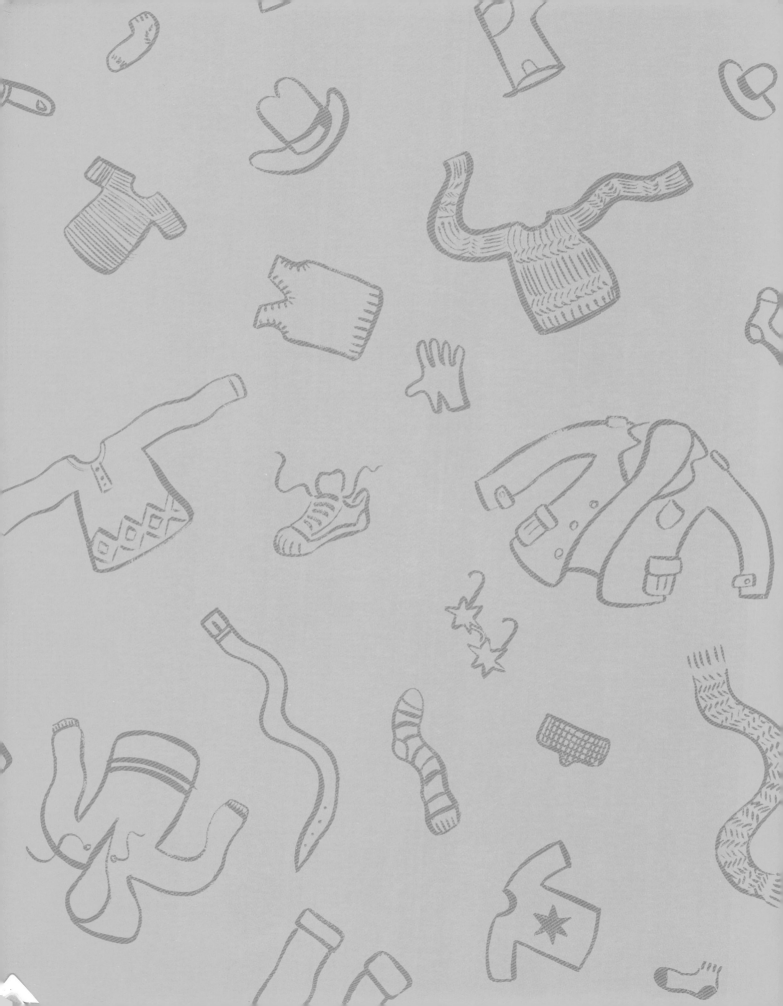